"You're the on[   ]
you?" he asked.

"Yeah," I said, surprised and unnerved that he and I were actually thinking about the same thing. "But everything is fine. Race has never been a problem."

"You also belong to that club of girls who do all those goody-goody jobs, don't you?"

I nodded. I didn't like him talking about the Kids Care Club that way, making us sound like a bunch of wimps.

"All those members are white, too, aren't they?"

"So what?" I said, defensively. "They're my friends, and I like them."

He looked around to see if anybody was near us. Unfortunately we were completely alone.

He leaned real close and hissed in my face, "Why don't you stop hanging out with white people, Alysha? It's time you learned to be what you really are. It's time you learned to be black!"

The East Edge Mysteries
- The Secret of the Burning House
- Discovery at Denny's Deli
- Mystery at Harmony Hill
- The Case of the Missing Melody
- The Mystery of the Poison Pen

THE MYSTERY OF THE
POISON PEN

GAYLE ROPER

Chariot Books™
A Division of Cook Communications

Chariot Books™ is an imprint of David C. Cook Publishing Co.
David C. Cook Publishing Co., Elgin, Illinois 60120
David C. Cook Publishing Co., Weston, Ontario
Nova Distribution, Ltd., Eastbourne, England

THE MYSTERY OF THE POISON PEN
© 1994 by Gayle Roper

Cover design by Helen Lannis and Chris Dall
Cover illustration by Cindy Weber
First printing, 1994
Printed in the United States of America
98 97 96 95 94   5 4 3 2 1

Library of Congress Cataloging-in-Publication Data

Roper, Gayle G.
       The mystery of the poison pen / Gayle Roper.
              p.   cm. -- (East Edge mysteries; #5)
       Summary: Twelve-year-old Alysha, an African-American, is appalled that someone in her church would leave poison pen notes about a baby with AIDS, and is determined to find the culprit, while also facing more subtle forms of prejudice from her white friends, her cousin, and her new gymnastics coach.
       ISBN 0-7814-1507-1
       [1. Prejudices--Fiction. 2. Conduct of life--Fiction. 3. Christian life--Fiction. 4. Gymnastics--Fiction. 5. AIDS (Diseases)--Fiction. 6. Afro-Americans--Fiction. 7. Mystery and detective stories.] I. Title. II. Series:
Roper, Gayle G. East Edge mysteries ; #5.
PZ7.R6788Pu 1994
[Fic]--dc20

                                                              94-6755
                                                                CIP

For Skip and Joann
With thanks to
Ruth and Tori and Eileen

"Just imagine how many little kids have slobbered over this thing," said Bethany. She plunged a rubber duck into the sink of sudsy water, where a couple of plastic cars were already floating. "It's enough to make me gag."

I looked at the toy in my hands, a playhouse that opened in the middle so a kid could put little people inside it. It was tattletale gray from use.

Bethany and I were at Calvary Church in East Edge, Pennsylvania, this Friday afternoon in September with the other girls from our sixth-grade Sunday school class. We were cleaning the nursery and toddler room—a project our teacher, Gail Macklinburg, had gotten us involved in.

Usually we girls find our own work as members

of the Kids Care Club. We do jobs for people and give part of the money to the church's Help Fund. But today was Gail's project, and there was no money involved.

"We'll just be helping people and serving the Lord," Gail said last Sunday when she told us about it. "The room needs cleaning to get rid of all the germs. It's important for mothers to know they can leave their children without worrying about sickness."

Gail's a nurse, and she worries about things like germs and disease. We girls all feel it's time she stopped thinking about health and started thinking about a husband and kids and stuff. She may be beautiful with her dark hair and eyes, but she's twenty-eight and isn't getting any younger.

"And after we're finished," Gail had added last Sunday, "we'll have a pizza party at my place."

"With dessert from Mr. Jack's?" we all asked.

Mr. Jack owns a bakery down the street from church, and he makes the best cakes and cookies and pies and rolls and muffins you ever ate. My favorites are Mr. Jack's chocolate eclairs and his huge chocolate chip cookies. The cookies are each as big as a dinner plate.

Gail nodded. "With dessert from Mr. Jack's."

We all like Gail a lot, and I like to go to her town house for pizza or any other reason. It's the kind of house I want to have when I become a world-famous gymnast. I intend to be a national champion first, then an Olympic gold medalist, which is how I'll become world-famous. I know it'll take a couple more years, but I'm willing to put in the time and sweat.

"Alysha," Gail called to me now, "here are the people that go with your house."

I took them from her and wondered, not for the first time, who had thought up these strange-looking people. No necks. No arms. No legs. Just round heads, round bodies, and round bottoms that fit in little circles on toys of all kinds. I guess the good thing about them is that they are easy for little kids to hold.

"You can put the people in the water," Gail said, "but don't put the house in. Just wipe it off well with a damp rag."

I walked away without saying anything, but I sometimes wonder if people think I'm stupid or something just because I'm small for my age. I mean, who would put a house into the water? It would be ruined.

I dipped a cloth into Bethany's soapy water and

began washing down the house. I remembered having one just like it when I was a kid. I looked closely. Maybe this one was mine, and my mother had given it to the nursery when I stopped playing with it. It would be just like her.

I remembered scribbling on the side of my toy house with Dad's pen, but this one had no ink marks. It had a few teeth holes and a ding or two from where some kid had thrown it or kicked it, but no scribbles. It wasn't mine.

I was genuinely surprised, because Mom gives anything and everything away.

"We have so much and others have so little," she always says.

"That's true," Dad always answers. "But I'd like to wear a shirt more than once before it disappears forever."

It's so bad that we have a saying around our house: *If you like it, hide it before Mom gives it away when you're not looking.*

"Alysha, you're not listening to me!" Bethany scowled, a look she uses to intimidate people.

"Sorry," I said, smiling as I dried the house. I was not about to be intimidated. "I was concentrating on what I was doing."

Bethany looked at me doubtfully. "Since when

have you started doing or thinking about only one thing at a time?"

It's a joke among my friends that I'm always thinking about lots of things at once. They're right; I usually am. I can't help it if I have an IQ of 140.

"There are times I only think about one thing," I said. "I think about one thing when I'm on the—"

"When you're on the uneven bars," Bethany cut in. "Or the balance beam. Or the horse."

I may have the habit of thinking about lots of things at the same time, but Bethany has the habit of finishing people's sentences for them. I'll take my habit over hers any day. At least mine doesn't make people mad.

In the nursery Dee was washing off the baby swings, and Shannon was cleaning off the changing table. Charlie and Cammi were washing down the cribs. Brooke, rich, stuck on herself, and totally unused to work, was trying to put clean sheets on the crib mattresses. She was having a hard time getting all those little fitted corners in place.

I was surprised that Brooke had even showed up for a workday. It didn't seem her style. Gail had probably told Mrs. Picardy about the project, and she had told Brooke she was going whether she wanted to or not. I always wondered how a nice woman like Mrs. Picardy had a daughter like Brooke.

Of course Brooke was the only one of us who came dressed to clean in a ruffled blouse and skirt and flats. The rest of us had on old clothes. She was also the only one trying to protect a manicure and keep her perfectly curled hair from getting messed up.

All the time I was thinking about Brooke, I was listening to Bethany, who was talking about family sizes.

"I knew a family once that had eight kids," she said. "You'd have thought it would be chaos all the time, but their mother kept them all organized. The main thing I didn't like was that she made them all have peanut butter and jelly sandwiches almost every day. On the other days they had to eat bologna and cheese. She didn't care whether they liked those things or not. She said anything else was too expensive. Do you think that a family can be too big?"

Of course, she didn't wait for an answer. That's another of Bethany's habits.

Around my house I'm never allowed to chatter

like Bethany. My mother won't stand for it.

"Dominating a conversation is impolite, Alysha," she always says. "Just because you know more than most people is no reason to be rude."

She's right.

"And remember," my father always adds, "that there's an extra burden to be kind for two reasons. One, you're a Christian. Two, you're a black child in a white world. Neither makes you inferior. It just requires extra diligence if you are to be a good model of both."

I don't worry much about being a good model, but it is nice to have people like you. So I try to watch that I don't talk just to talk. I think it's a shame, though, that Bethany's parents never gave her the same lecture.

By the time Bethany finished talking about large families and had washed the trucks and the rubber duck, I'd finished the house, a barn, a garage, an airport, a McDonald's stand, and all their people. I put them carefully on the shelf that Gail had just wiped off.

"Alysha, it's almost 4:45," Gail said as I lined up the little people like a marching army.

"Oh!" I'd lost complete track of the time. "Thanks. Come on, Bethany," I called. "Time to go."

Bethany came, grumbling. She wanted to stay for the pizza party, and her wishes weren't helped any when we met Mr. Jack himself in the hall carrying two big boxes of delicious-smelling goodies.

"Oh, no," groaned Bethany. I could hear her stomach growling.

I felt the same way, but we couldn't stay, no matter how good the pastries smelled or how much fun it was to go to Gail's. We had practice.

"Are you two leaving?" Mr. Jack asked.

We nodded. I was trying not to drool as I inhaled the wonderful aroma of freshly baked goodies.

"Practice," I explained.

He nodded. "Then you need energy." And he reached into a box and brought out two of his marvelous cookies.

"Oh, thank you!" Bethany and I said in perfect unison.

"No problem," said Mr. Jack. "They'll never miss them." And he went to find Gail and the others.

We hurried down the hall to the front door where Mom would be waiting to drive us to the gym, clutching our cookies like the treasures they were.

14

"Your mom's bringing us something to eat, isn't she?" Bethany asked around her mouthful of cookie. "I certainly need more than this. But not peanut butter and jelly or bologna and cheese, I hope. Of course nothing will taste as good as the pizza at Gail's would have." She sounded as though she'd never have a chance to eat pizza again in her whole life.

I looked at Bethany and wondered if she was getting ready to quit gymnastics. I'd noticed before that some girls wanted out when they got to be about twelve or thirteen or fourteen. Sometimes they left because they discovered boys. Sometimes they just got tired of the four hours of practice five nights a week. Sometimes their bodies made continuing hard.

If Bethany left, it would be for the last reason. She'd always been sort of stocky, but she'd been a good gymnast anyway. But she was maturing early. She had zits and braces and was rapidly developing a chest. As any gymnast knows, a fast-growing chest can throw your balance all out of whack.

We banged out the front door just as Mom pulled into the lot. When the door swung wide, a single sheet of paper that had been fastened to it slipped to the ground.

I stooped and picked it up and automatically read it.

> *Denning —*
> *Get that kid out of here before she kills*
> *someone! I'm warning you!*

I stared at the paper, trying to decide why anyone would send Dee Denning either a stupid joke or a nasty threat.

"Better give it to Dee," said Bethany, who had been reading over my shoulder. "She'll know what it's all about."

I waved at Mom to let her know I'd be right back, and Bethany and I ran back to the nursery, passing an empty-handed Mr. Jack as we went.

"Coming back for another cookie?" he called after us.

"Not a bad idea," Bethany muttered in my ear.

"Hey, Dee," I called as we rushed into the nursery and came to a stop beside Mr. Jack's boxes of wonders. "Here's—"

"—a note for you," finished Bethany.

Dee is our pastor's daughter and the president of the Kids Care Club even though she's almost the newest kid around. She's president because the club was her idea and because she's a good organizer.

Dee read the note aloud: "Denning—Get that kid out of here before she kills someone! I'm warning you!"

She looked up, her face slightly shocked. "What kid?" she asked. "Who's going to kill someone?"

Suddenly I understood the note. Gail understood at the same time, and we turned toward Charlie.

Charlie Fowler is the newest kid around. She's a bit rough around the edges in things like manners and people skills, but that's because her mom ignored her right up until the day she finally deserted the girl for good. Now Charlie's a foster daughter to Mr. and Mrs. Anderson who go to Calvary Church.

When she saw us look at her, she backed up, looking scared. She understood the note too, and she didn't know us well enough yet to know how we would react.

One by one the rest of the girls caught on and

turned toward Charlie.

"Don't worry, Charlie," Gail said. "It'll be all right."

Charlie didn't look convinced.

I went and stood beside Charlie. So did Bethany, a large chocolate chip cookie in her hand, one bite taken. How could she raid Mr. Jack's pastry boxes for another cookie at a time like this?

Shannon walked over and patted Charlie's arm and said, "We won't let anything happen to her." Shannon had been Charlie's first East Edge friend.

Charlie still didn't look convinced, but she looked less scared.

"I think we need to speak with Pastor Denning," said Gail.

"Dad's still here," Dee said. "He's working late tonight because he was out of the office all day yesterday at some meeting in Philadelphia. He told Mom not to have dinner until seven."

All of us trooped down the hall to the pastor's office. He looked a bit surprised when we all walked in, but he welcomed us just as if we were important adults.

Dee handed her dad the note.

I watched him read it and saw his lips press

together in distress.

Then he looked up at us and searched our faces. He could see that we understood exactly what the note meant.

"It'll be all right, Charlie," he said. "Nasty things like this—"and he waved the note—"won't stop us from doing what's right."

"It's just that she's so little," said Charlie. "It makes me so sad!"

"And mad," I said. "Picking on—"

"—a baby!" finished Bethany.

Pastor Denning nodded. "I feel exactly the same way. But the church elders and I have talked a lot about Melody, and we expected that there might be some people foolish enough to act like this." Again he waved the note.

Melody is Charlie's foster sister. She's six months old, and she's HIV-positive. She caught the disease from her birth mother who was an intravenous drug user. Melody doesn't have AIDS yet, but she's contagious. Charlie's not allowed to help her if she bleeds or anything, because body fluids carry the germs. If she breathes on you or kisses you, though, that's no problem.

The main reason we were cleaning the nursery was because Melody had been in there before she was diagnosed, and we wanted to make certain it was safe for all the babies and toddlers.

Melody is the cutest little thing you ever saw. She always smiles and coos, and she loves everybody, especially Charlie. She looks so cute because she has blonde hair that's black on the tips. Charlie calls it her reverse dye job.

Everybody knows Melody is HIV-positive because she was kidnapped recently, and it was reported in the newspaper.

"What are you going to do, Dad?" asked Dee.

Pastor Denning took a deep breath. "We don't have everything figured out yet, but we do know Melody can't go back to the nursery because of all the other babies and kids. Little people her age chew and slobber and mess so much that we can't protect the kids and the workers from the danger."

"It's not fair," Charlie said.

"You're right," Pastor Denning agreed. "But there's nothing else we can do when we have to consider so many people. We've told Mrs. Anderson that she's certainly welcome to bring Melody to church. It's only the nursery that's a problem."

"Won't the baby ever be allowed to be with the rest of the kids?" I asked. I didn't say it, but I was wondering how she would ever grow up to have friends and be normal if she could never play with other kids.

"When she's older and doesn't bite her friends, then things will probably be different." He smiled so we'd know he was making a joke.

That didn't make me feel much better. I understood what he was saying—I just didn't like it.

"And as far as finding out who wrote the note," he continued, "we'll look into it."

Adult talk for not having an answer yet, I thought.

We left the office soon after that, and I found myself walking beside Brooke. Her curls looked a bit straggly, and her ruffles were a little grungy around the edges, presumably from all her hard work putting sheets on the cribs. It cheered me a bit to see her looking slightly imperfect.

"I think it's best if Melody just stays home," she said seriously. "Even sitting in the church is too dangerous. I don't want to get AIDS just so some kid can come to church!"

"Brooke!" I was appalled at her attitude. I mean, I certainly don't want to get AIDS either, but that was no reason to be mean to Melody. It's not her fault she's sick.

Brooke saw my face. "Don't get all righteous with me!" she snapped. "Who wants an infectious kid around?" And she stalked away in a huff.

3

EAST EDGE KIDS CARE CLUB

"Mom," I said after Bethany and I were finally on our way to practice, "she wants Melody to stay home all the time!"

Mom nodded. "I imagine she's not the only one."

"But that's terrible! It's not right! And it means Mrs. Anderson would have to stay home all the time too. And she didn't do anything wrong either!"

"People are scared," said Mom. "They don't want to get sick, and they don't want their kids to get sick. Especially since there's no cure."

"But it's rotten!" I said. "The whole situation is rotten!"

Mom nodded her head. "That's true.

Sometimes life is rotten, honey."

"But that doesn't mean we just give up! There's got to be a way to keep all the little kids safe and make things fair for Melody."

Mom didn't say anything more, but I knew what she was thinking.

"Alysha, you amaze me," she often says. "You get worked up over everything, and you want to fix everything. Even more amazing is the fact that you often do figure out some way to solve the problem."

Well, I'd figure out something this time too! My mind was going so fast, looking for ways to help, that Bethany had to pull me from the car when we got to the gym.

"We're here, Alysha," she said. "Time to forget Melody for a while. Besides,"—her voice got quiet and sad—"there are some situations that aren't fixable."

I sniffed and shook my head. "Not so," I said, but deep down I was afraid she was right.

I walked inside, and instantly Melody receded. I love coming to the gym, even on a hot, sticky day like today. The smell, terrible to most people, is perfume to me. It means sweat and hard work and good times. I've never been able to figure out how people who don't come to the gym have fun or what they do with their time.

Raisor's Gym has huge garage doors all along one wall because the building was supposed to be a trucking warehouse. The doors were all open today, trying vainly to make the place cool.

The floor of the gym is stuffed full of equipment including nine balance beams of various heights, a couple of vaulting horses, a large area with a mat for floor exercises, several sets of uneven bars, and a few high bars that the men do their routines on. Everything in the area of the bars is covered with a fine snowfall of white chalk dust.

One of my favorite places is the pit full of chunks of foam rubber about the size of our bathroom wastebasket. This pit is just behind one of the vaults. When we were kids, they'd let us climb around in the foam if we were good. Now we use it to land in when we're practicing a new vault. It's a lot more forgiving than the hard floor when we mess up.

There's a balcony that probably would be used for offices if a trucking firm actually used the building. That's where we do our stretching and have our ballet classes.

We dashed up the stairs to the balcony and pulled off our outer clothes. I bent and stretched my legs for a minute before I placed my right heel on a foam support about eighteen inches high. I slid my left foot as far behind me as I could, lowering myself into a split.

"Nice you finally showed up," said Morgan as she lowered herself into a split beside me. "Mrs. Sessions was looking for you."

"Who's Mrs. Sessions?" I asked.

"She's our coach for the next week or two until Mr. Raisor comes back from vacation," Morgan said.

I made a face. "I hate substitute coaches. They never know what you're supposed to be doing."

Bethany took Morgan's back leg and lifted it gently off the floor a couple of inches. We have to be able to extend beyond a regular split so we won't get injured if something goes wrong during a routine.

Sasha began working on my legs. "Mrs. Sessions wasn't happy about not finding you." Her voice took on a high, snotty tone, " 'Aren't we missing someone? Where are those two late delinquents?' "

I grinned. Sasha doesn't just mimic people, she creates whole personalities with her voice and face and hands.

27

Morgan and Sasha have been in gymnastics with Bethany and me since we were all four years old. I like both of them a lot, not only because they're funny but because they're as set on being world class as I am. We all have to work very hard not to let the others pass us by. Morgan and I are Level 10 gymnasts, Sasha is Level 9 because she hates the uneven bars and keeps messing up on them, and Bethany is Level 8. We're the youngest girls on the senior team. The other eight are in junior or senior high, so the four of us hang together.

Sasha is a small girl like me, and has blonde curls all over her head. I often wonder what it's like to have curls that aren't tight, tight like mine. Morgan is taller than me and Sasha and even Bethany, and she has real long legs. If she lets her hair hang long, she can sit on it, but she always wears it pulled back and knotted for the gym. I can't imagine taking care of that much hair. It's bad enough dealing with mine, and it's only long enough to pull back out of my way.

"Well," said a pleasant voice that, fortunately, didn't sound a bit like Sasha's imitation. "And who have we here?"

A very sturdy-looking woman with the build of

a professional wrestler—I figured she must be Mrs. Sessions—smiled at us.

Bethany and I scrambled to our feet and gave our names.

"I'm sorry we were late," I said. Some coaches get very upset about lateness, and others are willing to give some slack. I had no idea which kind Mrs. Sessions was.

Bethany nodded. "Alysha's mom wasn't really late—"

Mrs. Sessions nodded. "I see."

Bethany and I looked at each other. What did she see? We hadn't told her anything yet.

"Try not to let it happen again. And, Bethany, take off that T-shirt."

Bethany groaned as she pulled her shirt off. Its logo read, *If you can't do gymnastics, play football*. It was Mr. Raisor's idea of a joke, and he loved to give the T-shirt to all his old college buddies who were football coaches.

"Told you you'd have to get rid of it," I whispered as she tossed the shirt in the general direction of her gym bag. Since she'd started getting her prominent chest, she hated wearing just her leotard. She felt too exposed, I guess. But a T-shirt or anything at all! loose or baggy is dangerous around the equipment. If it caught on something, you could be thrown off balance or off stride and get badly hurt.

"Leotards and that's it," Mr. Raisor always says. "I care for you all too much to be lenient about this rule."

Morgan lay on her stomach and kicked her legs up and over her head until she looked like a big C. I pushed down gently on her legs, and the C became more and more like a sideways U.

After I took my turn doing the same thing, I sat on the floor, leaning back on my elbow. I lifted my legs off the floor and made the widest sideways split I could. Morgan put her hands on the inside of my knees and began to push.

After a half hour of flexibility work, we went downstairs for a half hour of conditioning. I checked the posted list of exercises we were to do and was pleased that we weren't lifting weights. Tonight our exercises included chin-ups on the bars, body lifts while hanging from our knees, and push-ups from handstands. I spotted for Morgan and she spotted for me as we worked our way through the required moves.

Then came rotations of forty-five minutes on each of the four disciplines. When I said I rarely thought of anything but the discipline I was working on, I was being very serious. I knew it was especially necessary to concentrate the first couple of weeks after school started. All summer I had worked on new skills, and now, just when I felt I was making good progress, school came along and sapped my energy. Throwing my new tumbling run suddenly seemed more than I could do.

The balance beam is my favorite piece of apparatus, and it's become my specialty. I'd spend all night on it if I could. I was learning to do a back handspring and two layouts.

Look for the beam, I told myself as I began. The only way you can land on that narrow piece of wood is to spot the beam behind and below as soon as you can. I spend a lot of time picking myself up off the floor.

I like the horse least, so I work on it very hard. The uneven parallel bars are fun, and I like the floor exercise. I wish I were more elegant on the floor, but I think my size and bounciness have sentenced me to be a pixie forever.

Mrs. Sessions traveled with us from apparatus to apparatus, making suggestions and giving encouragement. She didn't know where we were individually or what we were supposed to be doing except in the most general terms, but she obviously knew gymnastics. I wondered where Mr. Raisor had found her.

"Morgan, head up," she called. "And back straight."

Morgan's posture improved immediately.

"Bethany, extension! Get those arms up!"

"I'm extended," Bethany mumbled grumpily.

"No, you're not," Mrs. Sessions said. What ears the woman had! "Reach for the ceiling!"

And somehow Bethany reached higher, and her movements looked cleaner.

"That's the way to approach the vault, Sasha! Keep up that speed!"

"For a substitute," said Bethany on the way home, "she's not too bad. She had some good advice for me on the beam."

It wasn't till later that I realized that Mrs. Sessions hadn't given *me* any good advice. In fact, she hadn't spoken to me since our introduction.

How strange.

EAST EDGE
4
KIDS CARE CLUB

"Hurry up and get your breakfast, Alysha,"
Mom called. "I don't want to be late."

I climbed into my favorite purple leotard, some
black shorts, and a T-shirt, and ran downstairs.

It was Saturday morning, and Mom was going
to an emergency meeting of all the Sunday school
teachers at nine. I had to go along if I wanted her
to get me to the gym at ten. Even then she'd
probably have to leave her meeting early to take
me.

Mom's very good about seeing I get to the gym
whenever I need to be there. She works here at
home on her own computer setup, editing books
for a local publisher. She used to be a full-time
editor before I was born, going into the office and

stuff. Now she works at home because she likes to be here if we need her.

I think she works as hard as she does because she needs the money for me. Gymnastics is very, very expensive. I used to feel guilty about that, but now I realize that she likes her work, so it's not *only* for me that she does it.

I sat down for breakfast with Mom and Dad and my little brothers, Damon who's seven and Thetis who's four. Also at the table were my little cousins Mbasa and Batutta, who live down the street from us. Aunt Thea named the kids when she was in her back-to-our-roots phase. I always feel sorry for them because I know what it's like to have to spell your name for everybody. At least mine sounds normal. They must have a terrible time.

We Jacksons all live in the same neighborhood. There's the five of us in our little family; Aunt Thea and Uncle Bud and Mbasa, Batutta, and Kenya; Uncle James and Aunt Arlette and their five kids; Uncle Tug, who's not married; and Aunt Beedee and Uncle Louis, who have no kids because they just got married. And of course Grandma and Grandpa Jackson.

We all get together every Sunday after church

34

for a big family dinner at somebody's house. We always used to go to Grandma Jackson's, but she's been sick lately. She has edema real bad, and her feet swell so she can't stand long enough to cook for all of us anymore.

So now we rotate houses. It's fun, and I like most of my cousins a lot in spite of some of their names. One or two I'd be glad to trade with another family, any other family, but I'm always glad I'm a Jackson.

Mbasa and Batutta are nice little kids, and they're here all the time playing with Damon and Thetis.

"We've got a substitute coach while Mr. Raisor's on vacation," I told everybody over the eggs Mom had scrambled. "Her name's Mrs. Sessions, and she never spoke a word to me yesterday."

"Weird," said Damon.

"Just my thought," I said.

"Was she unkind?" asked Dad.

"Or mean?" asked Mom.

I knew what they were thinking. "You mean because I'm the only black kid in the gym?"

They nodded. Mom and Dad are great about helping us be proud of ourselves, but they're also aware that there are people out there who think being black is a disease or something. They've warned us, and they try to help us if we bump into this kind of person.

I shook my head. "She didn't seem prejudiced or anything," I said. "I've seen it at school a couple of times in kids who don't want to sit next to me or something. But Mrs. Sessions didn't treat me like that. It was as if—" I stopped a minute to think how to explain it. "It was as if I wasn't even there."

"Sometimes I wish you weren't here," said Damon as he swayed back and forth in his seat. Damon never sits still. It's sway, sway, sway, sort of like he's always sailing on a very rough ocean.

Come to think of it, Thetis never stays still either. He bounces all the time, as though he has springs on his feet. Boing, boing, boing!

I don't know how my parents stand it.

"Sometimes I wish you weren't here either," I told Damon as I buttered another piece of toast. "Especially when you grab the last Coke or Tastykake or something. But that's not because you're black, kid. It's because you're my little brother, and I'm stuck with you."

"I know what the problem was with that lady," said Thetis, smiling his wonderful smile. "She was

36

so impressed with how good you are that she couldn't think of anything to say."

"Piffle," I said, but I smiled at him because he meant every word and because he's the cutest kid in the world. I ignored the hoots from Damon and the cousins.

Mom went to the meeting with all the other Sunday school teachers while I wandered the halls, killing time. I checked the nursery, and it practically sparkled. The girls and Gail had finished things up very nicely.

"Hey, Alysha. How are you doing, sweetheart?"

I turned around to see Uncle James walking down the hall, broom in hand. Uncle James is the church sexton, and he keeps things neat and clean. He's one of my favorite uncles.

"Your mom in that meeting learning all that the church is going to do about people with AIDS?" he asked.

"Is that what the meeting's about?" I wasn't surprised.

"Yup. Lots of people in there too. Gail's doing a lot of the talking, I think."

I nodded. "Because she's a nurse."

"These are tough times, baby," Uncle James said, shaking his head at the toughness of it all.

37

"What do you think they should do about Melody?" I asked.

"I don't know what I think, honey," Uncle James said, "I can see both sides of the issue too clearly. She can't put people in danger, but she needs to have some kind of a normal life too."

"I think we've got to be nice to Melody," I said. "The Bible tells us to love one another, and not just when we're well."

Uncle James grinned at me. "Always the tiger," he said, punching me lightly on the shoulder.

"I don't want to be a tiger," I said. "I just want to do what's right."

"Hey, Dad!" The voice of my cousin Edward echoed down the hall. Edward is fourteen and one of the cousins I could live without. "Look what I found!"

Uncle James held his finger to his lips for Edward to be quiet.

Edward, as usual, ignored him. "Look, Dad!"

A bull moose bellowing before a battle is probably quieter than Edward.

Uncle James hurried down the hall toward Edward and I followed. I didn't have anything better to do.

"Edward," said Uncle James, "keep your voice

38

down. There's a meeting going on."

Edward looked blank. "So?"

"So we don't want to disturb them."

"If they don't want to be disturbed, then they shouldn't meet when you're working," Edward said.

I looked at him and wondered why I had to be related to such an idiot. "I don't think it's your father who's making the noise," I said.

"So?"

Someday I'm going to give him a thimble because he says "So?" so often. Trouble is that I don't think he'd get the joke.

"So shut up," I said.

"Come on, you two," Uncle James said. "Enough. What was it you wanted to show me, Edward?"

Edward held out a piece of paper. Uncle James and I read the large, sloppy printing at the same time.

> *Denning—*
> *Remember my warning. Get rid of that*
> *kid before it's too late!*

"Another one," I said, feeling weird all over.

"Another?" said Uncle James and Edward at the same time.

"Someone wrote one yesterday, too. Bethany and I found it taped to the front door."

"That's where I found this!" Edward was excited.

"I think we'd better take it to Pastor Denning," Uncle James said.

We walked to the pastor's office. The door was open, but he wasn't there.

"I bet he's in the meeting," I said.

Edward looked at his father. "We can't wait around until some meeting's over, Dad. You know that."

"Why not? Where are you going?" I asked.

"I've got a drill team competition today in Bethlehem. I got excused from riding the team bus because my family's coming, but I can't be late!"

"Don't worry, Edward," said Uncle James. "I'll go get Pastor from his meeting."

Uncle James placed the note in the middle of Pastor Denning's desk, then he left the room. Edward trailed after him.

I stayed, looking at the note, trying to imagine what kind of a person would write something like that. I mean, who threatens ministers? And over babies?

I noticed the corner of the first note sticking

out from under some books on Pastor Denning's desk. I slid it out and laid it beside today's note.

The same person had written them, there was no doubt about it. The paper and the ink and the printing were just the same.

I studied the sheets closely. The paper looked like it was taken from a packet of three-ring binder paper, the kind that's sold in K Mart and Jamesway and every other store in America. The pen was probably a Bic pen, the kind you can buy at Wal-Mart and Rite Aid and every place else, too. The printing was that of an adult trying to look like a kid.

Suddenly I had an idea. I peered out of the office and saw with satisfaction that the hall was still empty. I grabbed the two notes, dashed to the secretary's office, and ran to the copier. I knew I couldn't have the original notes, but if I had copies. . . .

The machine wasn't on!

I searched for the right button and went through torture waiting for the copier to warm up.

What if they came back and found the notes—and me—gone?

I was just ready to give up and run back to the pastor's office before I got caught when the machine sang its little "I'm-ready" song. One second, two seconds, and I was finished. I flipped the machine off and ran.

I had note one under the stack of books when I realized I'd left note two in the machine. I had to go back to the secretary's office again.

I knew I was going to get caught before I got the second note back on the desk. I knew it. My heart was pounding and my palms were sweaty. My parents would never have to worry about my leading a life of crime. My nerves wouldn't be able to handle the stress.

I had just put note two back in the middle of the desk when I heard voices, and I stuffed my copies into my pocket as the men and Edward entered the room.

Pastor Denning looked at the note lying in the middle of his desk.

"I was afraid this would happen," he said. He pulled the first note out from under the books and placed it beside the new one.

The four of us stared at them.

"Nasty stuff," said Uncle James. "It looks like the same person."

Pastor Denning nodded. "Thank goodness. The last thing we need is a second poison pen."

"Have you had others make an issue about Melody?" asked Uncle James.

"Several have expressed concern," Pastor Denning said, "but most of them have been polite about it." The corner of his mouth curved up in a sad sort of smile, and I knew some had not been polite. "A couple of people have threatened to leave, depending on how we handle things. But no one else has stooped to this."

He stared at the notes, and I thought how tough it must be to be a pastor. How could you ever make all the people in your church happy at the same time, especially about something like Melody?

If he said she couldn't come anymore, then I'd be unhappy, and so would lots of others.

If he said she could continue to come, another group would be upset.

I decided I was very glad that Dad was a metallurgical engineer at Lukens Steel Company. At least steel couldn't talk back.

"Have you checked the notes for fingerprints?" asked Edward.

"No." Pastor Denning shook his head. "I've thought about it, but we don't want to involve the police."

"You could find them yourself," Edward said, all excited. "All you need is cellophane tape. Press it on, then lift it off. It'll bring prints with it."

"It'll just stick, Edward," I said. "Tape doesn't pull off paper without bringing up half the paper."

44

I tried to sound sarcastic, but my heart was racing. If they could lift prints, guess whose they'd find? I didn't think making my copies was exactly wrong, but I had sneaked because I knew the adults wouldn't do it for me.

Pastor Denning shoved both notes under his pile of books. "Even if we could get prints, Edward, we'd have no way of knowing whose we'd have. We can't have a church-wide fingerprint collection. No, we'll just have to solve this little mystery some other way."

He ran a hand through his hair, and I could see that he was one worried man.

"One thing I want to ask the three of you," he said. "Don't go telling lots of people about the notes. I know Alysha's friends all know about the first note, and of course the church leaders will have to know about them both. But don't tell uninvolved people. We haven't said anything to the people in the meeting"—he gestured down the hall—"about our poison-pen writer. We don't want to create more upset than there already is."

The three of us nodded.

"I've got to go back to my meeting. Thanks, James, for getting me." He and Uncle James shook hands, and Edward and I followed them out.

45

As the pastor walked away, Edward grabbed his father's sleeve.

"Dad, we got to go!"

"In a minute, son. I need to visit the men's room."

"So?"

"So you'll have to wait for me." Uncle James didn't keep the exasperation out of his voice. I was cheered that he felt the same way I did about Edward's "so's."

Edward looked at me. "We have a good chance of winning today," he said. If he'd seemed excited about the fingerprint idea, he was positively flying now. "We've been practicing all summer on some great routines."

I couldn't help myself. I looked at him and said, "So?"

He was not happy.

"Sorry, Edward," I said, and I was. I'm not usually sarcastic, but when I am, it's with Edward. When they talk about people who bring out the best in you, they aren't talking about Edward, believe me. But I wasn't going to lower myself to his level.

"I hope you do win," I said. " How many are there on your drill team?"

"Forty-eight guys march, and there are about twenty who are apprentices."

I was impressed. Even though Edward talked about his team all the time, I'd never realized there were so many involved.

"Are any of the guys girls?" I asked.

"Yeah," he said, obviously disgusted. "We have to have girls now, but I don't like it. It was better when it was all guys."

"Why?" I asked, miffed. "Can't the girls keep cadence?"

He ignored my question. "We used to be the Screaming Eagles, the East Edge All-Male Drill Team. Now we're just the East Edge Drill Team. We're talking *BLAH!* At least we're still all black."

I was surprised. "What if someone white wants to join?" I asked. "Aren't there laws or something that force you to take anyone?"

"Who's going to stop us?" he said. "It's bad enough having to let girls join."

"Don't you like white people?" I asked, thinking about all my white friends.

Edward shrugged. "Sure. Some are nice enough. I just don't want to march with them."

I thought for a minute about what would happen if I didn't want to go to the gym with

47

white girls. Whoa! There'd be no gymnastics.

"You're the only black girl at your gym, aren't you?" he asked.

"Yeah," I said, surprised and unnerved that he and I were actually thinking about the same thing. Next thing I knew, I'd start saying "So?" all the time. I shivered at this very scary thought. "But everything is fine at the gym. Race has never been a problem."

"You also belong to that club of girls who do all those goody-goody jobs, don't you?"

I nodded. I didn't like him talking about the Kids Care Club that way, making us sound like a bunch of wimps.

"All those members are white, too, aren't they?"

"So what?" I said, defensively. "They're my friends, and I like them."

He looked around to see if anybody was near us. Unfortunately we were completely alone.

He leaned real close and hissed in my face, "Why don't you stop hanging out with white people, Alysha? It's time you learned to be what you really are. It's time you learned to be black!"

I frowned, unhappy and uncomfortable.
"You're crazy, Edward."

He shook his head. "I'm not. But you are. Think about it, Alysha. How many of your friends are African Americans?"

My mind whirled. I know lots of great people who are black, but now that he pointed it out to me, I had to admit that all the people I hung out with were white.

"But I'm with white kids because they're where I am, not because I don't want to have black friends," I defended myself.

"Then maybe you're hanging out at the wrong places." Edward spoke as though he knew exactly what he was talking about.

I stared at him. I know my mouth was hanging open. I don't think I've ever been so surprised in my life.

"Edward, what are you saying? Do you mean I should stop coming to church and going to the gym because there are mostly white people there?" I had to be certain that he really meant something that drastic.

He nodded.

"But you come to church," I said, pointing out the place where he wasn't consistent.

He ignored my comment and the gaping hole in his argument. "Stick with your own kind,

Alysha. Never forget what the white man did to us."

"What the white man did to us? Come on, Edward!"

"It's history, Alysha," Edward said. "It's history."

"Where do you get these ideas?" I asked. "It's sure not from Uncle James and Aunt Arlette or the rest of the family. It must be from some of the kids on your drill team. Or you've got a weird teacher."

"It's not a matter of getting ideas," he said as if he were talking to a very small and not very bright child. "It's history."

"Sure it is," I said. After all, I'd been getting A's in history all my life, and I'm the one everyone always wants on their Trivial Pursuit team. "Long ago some white men who have been dead for years and years and years made slaves of our ancestors. But the white people living today never did that to us, Edward."

He just snorted.

"And another thing," I said. My mind was jumping, jumping, trying to counter his comments. "What about forgiveness? Aren't Christians, past and present, supposed to forgive wrongs done to them?"

"You don't have any ethnic pride!" he accused.

"Sure, I do," I said. "I'm proud to be African American, but I'm not going to blame Bethany and Charlie and Dee for slavery, for heaven's sake. I'm not going to stop going to Mr. Raisor's gym because a white man 300 years ago brought some Africans to America in chains."

"See?" said Edward. "You're already white inside."

I stared at him. "If I'm white inside, then so are my parents, and so are Grandma and Grandpa, and so are your mom and dad. And what about Martin Luther King and all he did to get blacks and whites together?"

"But life for the black man in America is hard." One thing about Edward, when he finally gets an idea, he's hard to budge.

"You're right," I agreed. "For lots of black people, life in America is hard. And maybe when I'm older than twelve, I'll be able to do something about it. But for right now, for you and me, Edward, life's not bad. We've got family. We've got friends. Our parents have jobs. We live in a nice neighborhood. We go to a great church. We go to good schools. There are some crazy white people out there, I agree, but fortunately I haven't met many of them."

"Give it time," he said. "You will."

"Maybe," I said. "Maybe. But for now, I'm going to keep my friends."

EAST EDGE
KIDS CARE CLUB
6

After Edward and Uncle James left, I checked my watch. Another ten minutes before Mom would be ready to leave. I sighed and walked outside.

I hated discussions about racial issues. I wanted people to get along as though black and white didn't exist. I wanted everybody to accept everybody, just the way I wanted everybody to accept Melody.

I guessed neither was going to happen easily.

I took a deep breath to calm myself and started to salivate. Mr. Jack's Bakery was filling the air with wonderful scents.

I glanced at my watch again and decided I had time to run there if I hurried.

I burst in the front door of Mr. Jack's and began looking at all the delicious things on the shelves behind the glass counters. Every single item looked wonderful.

"Thanks, Jack," said a large lady in a pair of jeans and a hot pink shirt. "Nobody makes them better."

Mr. Jack smiled.

A lot of people think Jack is Mr. Jack's first name, but it's not. It's his last. Jack's Bakery is like saying Felton's Shoes or Budinger Realty. Mr. Jack's first name is Harley, but nobody says, "Thanks, Harley. Nobody makes them better." It's always, "Thanks, Jack."

He doesn't seem to mind. I guess he's used to it.

"Hi, Mr. Jack," I said.

"Alysha." He beamed at me. "Let me guess. A chocolate eclair, right?"

I nodded.

"Is that all?" he asked as he slid one out of the case and into a little white bag.

"That's all." I took the bag and handed him some money. What better way to spend part of my allowance? "I just decided that eating an eclair would be the perfect way to wait for Mom to get out of her meeting."

"The meeting at church? Ah, yes," he said. "My wife's there too."

"I didn't know she taught Sunday school," I said, sliding my eclair out of its bag. I was starting to salivate, so I took a tiny nibble. A bite the size I wanted to take would've been too impolite for conversation. "What age does she work with?"

"Fifth graders," he said. "She loves it."

"My Sunday school teacher is in charge of the meeting," I said. "She's a nurse, and she's going to show everyone how to take what she calls universal precautions like using rubber gloves and stuff."

"You mean the meeting is about health issues?" Mr. Jack asked.

I nodded. "It's to teach the teachers what to do if they ever have a student with AIDS or any contagious disease, even a common cold."

Mr. Jack shook his head. "What has this world come to when it's not even safe to teach Sunday school?"

We looked at each other sadly for a minute. Then I glanced at the big clock on the wall, the one that looked like a wedding cake, and realized I was in very real danger of being late the second day in a row. I shoved my eclair back in the bag, waved good-bye, and ran.

I climbed in the car just as Mom came flying out the church door.

"Sorry I'm late," she said. "I didn't mean to stay so long."

"It's okay," I said. "I just got back from Mr. Jack's."

"So I see," said Mom as I stuffed the eclair into my mouth. It was heavenly. "He and Mrs. Jack brought a couple of trays of muffins and Danish to the meeting this morning."

"He's a nice guy," I said.

"He is," said Mom, "I just wish he'd come to church more often. Mrs. Jack comes every Sunday. He only comes once in a while. But he never fails to have baked goods available for any meeting."

I ate my eclair in silence for a minute. It was so good! When I was famous, maybe Mr. Jack would go around the world with me, baking whatever I wanted to eat whenever I wanted it.

When I finished my last bite and wiped my mouth, I asked the first of two questions that were on my mind.

"Mom, should white people stay only with whites?"

She looked at me, obviously wondering why I

was asking. "No, I don't think so. That exclusion creates prejudice and misunderstanding and keeps alive the unequal treatment too many have suffered."

I nodded. I knew she'd say that. "Well, what about blacks staying just with blacks?"

"I think that's just as wrong and creates just as much prejudice."

I nodded. I thought she'd say that. Now all I had to do was decide whether she was right, though I couldn't imagine disagreeing with her to agree with Edward.

"Why are you asking?" Mom said.

I shook my head. "No reason." I didn't want to tell her how stupid her nephew was.

When I went into the gym, I began my stretching by putting one foot beyond me, heel on the floor, and bouncing gently. Bethany was there, hiding in a T-shirt until Mrs. Sessions made her take it off. Sasha was bending and twisting like she was made of spaghetti, not bones and muscles. And Morgan was doing her splits and stretches with a grace I wished I had.

I stood on my hands and let my feet fall behind me to make a back bend. Then I walked up the wall until my feet were even with my waist. I was supposed to look like a sideways L, my arms, head, and chest straight up and down, my lower body and legs parallel to the floor.

I was doing this particular exercise because I could do it alone. I needed to think a bit more about what Edward had said. I stared at Bethany, Sasha, and Morgan. I looked at the other girls doing splits and deep knee bends at the ballet barre. It was amazing how strange they all looked upside down.

Did any of them think very much about the fact that I was black and they were white? Or were we just a close squad of gymnasts who supported and encouraged and challenged each other?

I wished Edward hadn't talked to me today.

I righted myself and was sliding down easily into a split when Mrs. Sessions walked up behind me and scared me half to death by booming in my ear. "Well, Alysha, I'm sorry that you were late again. Is this a pattern of yours?"

I felt cornered, so I tried to explain. "My mother was in a meeting—"

"Ah, yes," said Mrs. Sessions. "Your mother." And she walked away.

I looked at Bethany. "What's this 'Ah, yes, your mother' business?" I asked.

"Who knows?" she said.

We stretched in silence for a while. My feelings of strangeness had gone away some when Mrs. Sessions made her comment. Now it wasn't black against white. It was kid against adult. I was used to that, and I was on the same side as every kid here no matter what color each of us was.

"Guess what happened at church this morning?" I finally said.

"What?" said Bethany, seated with her legs spread and her forehead pressing toward the floor.

"Another note."

She sat up straight and stared at me. "Really?"

"Really."

"What'd it say?"

"Denning—remember my warning. Get rid of that kid before it's too late," I quoted.

"I wish I'd seen it!" she said.

I grinned. "I've got a copy of both."

Bethany stared at me. "They gave you a copy?"

"Well, not exactly," I said, brushing that point aside. "Want to see?"

I've probably never asked a more useless question in my life. She was dying to see. I got up, pulled my copies out of my gym bag and handed them over.

"Two notes in two days! I can't believe it!" she said, spreading them on the floor. "Where'd you find today's note?"

"I didn't find it, Edward did. It was tacked to the front door just like yesterday's."

Bethany studied the writing carefully. "They're obviously written by the same person."

"I think so too." I said as I looked at the notes over her shoulder. "By the way, Pastor Denning asked us not to say anything. He's afraid it'll make people upset."

"If Edward found the note, the whole world will know about it in no time."

"I hope not." I felt a little miffed at her comment about Edward. I could say or think anything I wanted about him. He was my cousin. Bethany should be a bit more careful—even though she was probably right.

I reached for the notes. I wanted to put them away before Mrs. Sessions saw them.

"What are you two looking at?" It was Sasha.

"There was another note," said Bethany, her eyes all excited.

I could have kicked her.

"Another note? About the baby? Morgan, there was another note!"

Morgan was balanced on one leg with the other extended as far and high behind her as she could get it. Her eyes got the same sparkly excitement as Bethany's and Sasha's. "What did it say?"

I looked at Bethany. "How do they know about the first note?" I hissed.

She blushed. "It just sort of slipped out. I mean, we're all friends and everything, and it's such a neat mystery."

"Don't worry," said Sasha. "We won't tell anyone. What did it say?"

"Denning—remember my warning. Get rid of that kid before it's too late," Bethany said. "Show her, Alysha."

I glared at her.

"You've got them?" Sasha was bouncing about just like Thetis. "Let me see!"

Bethany grabbed the papers from me and handed them to Sasha and Morgan. They read the notes eagerly.

"Same handwriting," said Sasha.

Bethany and I nodded.

"How are they ever going to find out who wrote them?" asked Morgan.

"Wish I knew," I said, taking the notes and stuffing them into my gym bag. The last thing I wanted was for Mrs. Sessions to see them.

"I've been thinking about this baby," said Sasha. "I remember reading about her in the papers when she was kidnapped, but I never saw a picture of her. How old is she?"

"Six months," I said. "And cute as can be."

"She has this little dimple in her left cheek," said Bethany.

"No, she doesn't," I said.

"Sure she does." But Bethany frowned. "Doesn't she?"

"Is she black?" Sasha asked.

"What?" I stared at her.

"I figured that if her mother did drugs and had AIDS and all, she was probably black."

"Sasha! I can't believe you said that! White people do drugs and have AIDS too!"

"Well, look at Magic Johnson," she said defensively. "And Arthur Ashe."

"Drugs didn't have anything to do with either of those men!" I was so mad. I hate it when people assume things! "Magic Johnson got AIDS through sex, and Arthur Ashe got it through a blood transfusion. He was an innocent victim!"

"Girls, girls!" Mrs. Sessions rushed up to us. "What are you doing talking in the middle of your workout? Alysha, stop it this instant and get to the business you came for. You know better than to disrupt the others as they work."

Disrupt the others as they work? I was furious. No one had yelled at me for being disruptive since first grade.

That unfortunate incident happened during the first week of school when Miss Wright thought that because I couldn't sit still, I wasn't paying attention. (Much as I hate to admit it, I used to be a lot like Damon and Thetis, all wiggly and squiggly.) Then Miss Wright learned that I heard everything she said and already knew it and anything else she cared to teach. After that she let me be squirmy as long as I kept my mouth shut.

And now Mrs. Sessions was accusing me of being disruptive. Me! What I wanted to know was why she thought *I* was the problem.

Bethany was the one who told what she shouldn't have.

Morgan was the one who was too interested.

Sasha was the one who made the uncalled-for comments.

And I got blamed!

It wasn't fair!

The four of us went silently to work on our flexibility requirements and then on to rotations. The atmosphere between us was heavy and dark. I caught Bethany and Sasha and Morgan looking at Mrs. Sessions, then looking at me, and then looking at each other, but none of them said anything. I guess they were afraid of getting yelled at. They also couldn't tell how angry I was.

I couldn't decide how angry I was either. I'd had an original surge of I-want-to-bite-your-head-off anger, but it had cooled. I was glad for the time to be quiet and think. I couldn't talk to anyone right then. I felt as though I had been run over.

God, I thought, *what's going on here? Help me to figure it all out.*

It was one of the only times gymnastics didn't drive every other thought from my mind.

By the time we got to the beam, I had thought through it all and come to some conclusions.

Bethany didn't know she should keep the note a secret. Pastor Denning hadn't said anything about silence to us girls yesterday. All Bethany knew was that we had a great mystery on our hands. Who wouldn't talk about that?

I knew Sasha didn't mean anything unkind by her comment. She had been my friend for years, and she was a kind person who never hurt anyone. And in some ways, her comments made sense because of the very public black figures who had AIDS.

And Morgan, poor Morgan, hadn't done anything at all wrong.

In a way the trouble had been my fault. I had reacted too quickly because I was upset at that jerk of an Edward.

As for Mrs. Sessions . . . I sighed. Who knew what was in her mind? I certainly didn't.

I began practicing my series on the beam. Without my even asking, Morgan stood next to the beam to spot for me. When I threw the final layout, she reached out and caught me by the waist to steady me so I wouldn't fall. It helped a lot.

"I'm sorry we got you into trouble," she said softly.

I nodded. "Don't worry. It wasn't your fault."

"Alysha," said Sasha from the next beam, "I'm sorry too. I didn't mean to upset you. I never want to upset anyone!"

"I know. It's okay. I overreacted."

Sasha smiled happily at me, and I thought again how much I liked her and Morgan—and Bethany and Dee and Charlie and all my white friends. Edward was crazy.

"Alysha, what am I doing wrong?" Sasha asked. She did a pair of layouts on her beam, losing her balance on the landing and falling off. She jumped back up and tried again. The same thing happened.

I looked at Morgan. "What do you think? Tentative landing?"

She nodded.

I turned back to Sasha. "You're scared you're not going to stick the landing, Sasha. You're holding your weight up in your shoulders, trying to be light on your feet. Don't do that. Hit the beam and push all your weight down. You'll be much more secure on your landing."

Sasha tried again, hitting the beam with a great thud. She wobbled a bit, but she didn't fall.

Mrs. Sessions looked at Sasha just in time to see

her improved performance.

"Very nice, Sasha," she said. "Do you know what you did differently?"

"Yep. I followed Alysha's advice."

Mrs. Sessions looked at me. "Alysha's advice?"

"Yep." Sasha seemed unaware of the instructor's surprise. "Next to Mr. Raisor, she gives the best advice."

"Alysha's third in the nation in beam, Mrs. Sessions." Bethany had come over to join us. "She's only fourth in floor, though. And Morgan's right behind her."

"Third on beam? Fourth on floor?" Mrs. Sessions was having a hard time understanding what Bethany was saying. She looked at me again. "What level are you, Alysha?"

"Level 10," I said. "I plan to test for Elite next year."

I could almost hear her mind going click, click, click as she upgraded her opinion of me. I was afraid to think about why it had been so low to begin with.

"How nice," she said weakly.

"You should see her compete, Mrs. Sessions," said Sasha. "She's a tiger."

"Very competitive," I agreed. "I hate—"

"—to lose," finished Bethany. "She just hates to lose."

Awkwardly Mrs. Sessions cleared her throat. "Okay, girls." She clapped her hands. "Let's get back to work. Alysha, show me what you're working on."

The rest of the time went quickly, and I had my rightful share of attention from Mrs. Sessions. While she appeared to be just as nice as she had been before, there was a difference. It was as if she was really seeing me for the first time. And she was a very good coach. I didn't know where Mr. Raisor had found her, but I was glad to have her help.

After practice I sat on the curb outside the gym and waited for Mom. I knew she had a lunch appointment with one of the writers she worked with, and she had told me she might be late. I pulled a book from my gym bag and began to read.

"Well, Alysha. Still here?" It was Mrs. Sessions on her way to her car.

I nodded. "Mom'll be late today, but I need to read this for school anyway." I held out *Time of Storm*, an autobiography I was reading for a book report due next month. "It's about the Holocaust."

"Are you a good student, Alysha?" Mrs.

Sessions asked. She was looking at me with great interest.

I nodded. "Very."

"A good student and a good gymnast."

I nodded. I didn't think it was the time to tell her I was good at everything I did. She'd probably think I was bragging, and I probably would be, trying to prove something to her.

"Be careful what you say about your abilities," Dad always says. "People won't understand."

"Will your mother be long?" Mrs. Sessions asked.

"I'm not sure," I said. "But I don't mind waiting."

"Maybe I could drop you off," she said. "Elwood Street isn't far out of my way."

I looked at her, frowning. Elwood Street? We didn't live anywhere near Elwood Street. I opened my mouth to tell her that when it hit me.

She thought I lived in the Elwood Street Housing Project!

Assumptions!

And I had been forgiving her for overlooking me in the gym!

I swallowed a couple of times so I could talk without my anger showing.

"Thank you, Mrs. Sessions, but we don't live near the Project. We live on Walnut Street, and I'm sure that's out of your way."

EAST EDGE KIDS CARE CLUB

8

Saturday night Dee and Charlie and I were flopped on my bed.

"Did you know there are sixty-three purple flowers in each stripe in the drapes?" I asked. "And sixty-two pink ones?"

I got up and walked to the window and stretched my curtains wide. "And twenty-seven stripes per panel. How many purple flowers all together?"

Charlie looked at me as though I was crazy. She didn't actually say "Who cares?", but she might as well have.

Dee shut her eyes and multiplied. "2402," she said.

"Almost. You forgot to carry the last 1. It's 3402."

My room is almost the way I wanted it, striped drapes and all. When I turned twelve, Mom told me she'd do whatever I liked.

"I want royal purple walls and rug," I said. "I want royal purple everything."

"Not on your life," she said. We settled for lavender walls and rug and a royal purple quilt. The drapes had just enough bright purple and pink to make me happy, though I would have preferred them to be all purple too.

"It's the color of royalty," I told Mom.

"It's the color of nightmares," she answered.

We were lying around passing time by counting flowers while our parents had a meeting. My father is chairman of the church's Board of Elders. Of course, Dee's father is pastor, and Charlie's foster parents were at the center of a poison-pen puzzle.

Three guesses what the meeting was about.

Down the hall Damon and Thetis were playing with Dee's eight-year-old twin brothers, Phil and Mike. You could hardly hear yourself think with all the noise they were making.

"I think they're bouncing each other off the walls," Dee said.

"I wouldn't be surprised," I said, standing on

my head and watching the clock to see how long it would be before I felt light-headed from all the blood rushing to my head. "None of them knows how to sit still."

"*They* don't know how to sit still?" Charlie said, looking at me.

"Of course they don't," I said. "Can't you hear them?"

"I think she's saying you can't sit still either," Dee said.

"Me?" I asked. I was beginning to feel slightly dizzy.

"You," said Dee.

I looked at her. "I'm still now, aren't I?"

"Well, yes," Dee conceded. "But it's hardly the usual still."

I looked back at the clock. I was approaching a new personal record. "So who do you think wrote them?" I said, referring to the poison-pen notes.

Charlie picked up the copies that had been lying on my bed. "I wish I knew. I'd like to give him a piece of my mind."

"Does your father know who wrote them, Dee?" I asked. I was just short of nausea, the blood pounding in my temples.

"I don't think so," Dee said. "Not that he'd tell

me even if he did know. He and Mom are very careful about what they let us kids hear."

"Charlie, come here a minute, please." It was Mrs. Anderson.

Charlie and Dee went downstairs right away. I stayed where I was until I thought I'd pass out and fall over. Then I lowered my feet and sat as still as a sleeping cat—Charlie should see me now, I thought—waiting for the black fuzzies to pass.

When I got downstairs, Mrs. Anderson stood in the living room with a bunch of papers in one hand and Melody on her hip.

"She's getting too whiny to keep with me in the meeting, Charlie. Will you play with her for a while?"

Charlie held out her arms, and Melody practically jumped into them. She grabbed a handful of Charlie's hair and began to chew it gurgling happily.

Mrs. Anderson put down her papers and picked up a diaper bag from the big blue chair by the front door. "All her things are in here, but call me if you need me."

Charlie nodded.

"Don't worry," said Dee. "We'll help."

"Who's worried?" said Charlie, hugging

Melody. "We're going to be just fine, aren't we, sweetie?"

Melody laughed, throwing her pudgy arms wide. Charlie's head, connected to the flying arms by her hair, jerked back.

"Hey! Take it easy, kid!" she said, rubbing her sore scalp. She tried to pry herself free, but Melody held on as though her fist was crazy-glued to Charlie's hair.

Mrs. Anderson smiled and went back to Dad's study, closing the door softly behind her.

She'd been gone about a minute when Melody gave a sneeze loud enough to drown out the little boys destroying the upstairs. Gunk streamed from her nose in a gross flood.

"Uh-oh," Dee said. She made a terrible face.

"I thought you said you were always going to be there for Charlie," I pointed our sweetly.

"I don't know," Dee said. "I don't mind blowing my own nose, but someone else's?" She shuddered.

"It's okay," said Charlie. "Just reach in the diaper bag and get out a pair of rubber gloves."

Dee pulled out gloves like the ones I've seen doctors and thieves wear on TV while Charlie sat on the sofa with Melody in her lap. Awkwardly

Charlie pulled the gloves on while Melody smiled and gurgled and ignored her green mustache.

"Tissues," Charlie said.

I ran to the powder room and brought back a box.

"Is mucus like that dangerous?" I asked. "I know body fluids carry the HIV virus, but does that mean all body fluids, even mucus or saliva or sweat?"

"The doctor told Mrs. Anderson that those things probably aren't very dangerous, but we should treat them as if they are, just in case."

Charlie took a tissue and wiped Melody's little nose while the baby struggled and twisted and complained loudly. Finally a clean face emerged from the struggle, and I reached out and took Melody.

Charlie held the dirty tissues in one hand and peeled that glove off over the tissues, sort of trapping them inside. Then she put the glove and tissues in her other hand and peeled that glove off over everything.

"You make a double layer of protection that way," she said. She reached inside the diaper bag and pulled out a plastic bag, put the gloves and tissue inside, and zipped it shut. Then she put the whole collection back in the diaper bag.

"I'm impressed," I said. "You did great!"

Charlie beamed. I don't think her mother ever complimented her much, so she loves it when anyone says something nice.

I put Melody on the floor and sat down beside her. Then I leaned my head back and clonked myself on the edge of something hard. I turned to look, and there were the papers Mrs. Anderson had set down. They were attached to a clipboard, which was what I had hit.

"Uh-oh," I said, reaching for the papers. "I bet she'll need these." I started to get up to take them to her, but I never got that far.

There on top of all the other papers on the clipboard was another letter from the poison-pen writer. This one wasn't addressed to Pastor Denning but to the Andersons.

Before I knew it, I had read it, and it was nasty.

*To the Andersons: You have no right to
bring that kid to church! Get rid of it or
stay home! We don't want you around!
We don't want that baby around!
Everybody agrees with me!*

"Did you know about this, Charlie?" I asked, holding out the clipboard.

"We shouldn't read that," said Dee. "It's not ours."

"I know," I said. "But I already saw it, and I can't unsee it. I couldn't help it, you know? I always read everything. It happened so fast, I didn't even realize until I was done."

Dee nodded.

"Besides," I said, "Mrs. Anderson left it here."

"What is it?" Charlie asked from her seat on the floor by Melody.

"A poison-pen letter to the Andersons telling them to keep Melody home." I read it out loud.

"Same paper?" Dee asked.

"Same paper," I answered. "Same pen. Same printing."

"Coward," said Charlie. She had tears in her eyes. "Whoever it is is a coward! He hasn't got the courage to talk to us face-to-face!"

"My mom says whoever it is is phobic," I said. "He or she is an AIDS-aphobe."

"I've got a phobia about spiders," said Dee. "I hate them. I break into a sweat if I even see one."

"But you don't go around writing poison letters to someone who happens to have spiders, do you?" I asked.

Dee shook her head. "There's no excuse to do

something this terrible."

"What? Who did what?"

The three of us spun around, and there stood Edward in the doorway.

"None of your business, Edward," I said.

"So?" he answered.

I shuddered. What a dufus! More to change the subject than because I wanted to know, I asked, "How did your competition go?"

He smiled with genuine pleasure. "We took second!"

"Congratulations. Now what do you want?"

"My mom sent me over because she can't get through on the phone. She thought it was probably you blabbing with one of your friends." He paused before the word friends so that the word was somehow dirty.

I glared at him. "Dad's having a business meeting. He's probably using the phone. I repeat, what do you want?"

"What's your mother having for dinner tomorrow? Mom wants to know so she can make the proper vegetable."

"I haven't got the vaguest idea," I said. "Anything will be fine."

"So you say." He looked down at me like I

couldn't possibly know what I was talking about. Suddenly he saw the board in my hand, and before I realized what he was going to do, he grabbed it and read the letter.

He whistled. "Another one, huh? Somebody's really mad!"

Melody had been staring earnestly at Edward when she screwed up her little face and sneezed mightily again.

"Yo!" shouted Edward. "Germs!" He backed away.

"Jerk," I muttered as I reached for the gloves and the tissues.

He watched in silence as I wiped the baby's nose and stripped off the gloves. "Do you have to do that all the time?" he asked.

Charlie nodded. "Or when she drools a lot or needs her diaper changed or when she throws up."

Edward was quiet for a minute. Then, "Maybe she should stay home," he said softly. "Maybe she really is dangerous."

I stared at him, outraged. "Edward," I said, "I'm ashamed of you!"

"So?"

Then a new thought hit me. "You didn't write these letters, did you?"

"Alysha!" said Dee, shocked. "You saw him just now. He was surprised when he read that note."

"Yeah?" I said. "Maybe he's just a good actor."

He narrowed his eyes and glared at me. "Alysha, you got nerve!" He turned and stalked out the door.

I noticed he hadn't answered me.

9

EAST EDGE KIDS CARE CLUB

Sunday was an interesting day. So many things happened that I could hardly believe it.

First of all, Mr. Jack came to church. I was standing near the front door after Sunday school, looking for my parents. They make us all sit together, and we meet at the same place each week because we all come from different Sunday school classes.

I wasn't paying much attention to all the people milling around when suddenly out of the corner of my eye, I saw Mr. Jack. He was looking around for Mrs. Jack, and when he saw me, he gave me a big wave.

He pushed his way over to me and said, "Alysha, my favorite pixie, how are you today?"

I grinned. I was glad he'd gotten someone to cover for him at the bakery. "Did you bring me an eclair?" I asked, knowing he hadn't. I mean, how could he?

"And risk being hated by everyone else because I didn't bring them one too?" He shook his head. "Too dangerous by far." Then he leaned close and said softly, like it was a big secret, "Drop in one day this week and I'll give you a chocolate chip cookie."

"Really? Give?" I could taste the crunchy sweetness already.

"Really," he said. "You're one of my favorite people. Ah, there's my wife. See you, kiddo." And with a wave he was gone.

I was still smiling when an absolutely unbelievable thing happened. Across the lobby the door opened, and who should walk through it but Mrs. Sessions. She stopped just inside and looked around the way you do when you've never been to a place before.

I had to look twice to be sure it was really Mrs. Sessions. At practice she wore biking shorts over a leotard and had her hair pulled back in a ponytail. Now she was dressed in a pretty flowered dress, and her hair was curled and hanging to her shoulders. She looked very nice.

But I didn't want to talk to her no matter how nice she looked. Before I even thought about how rude it was, I turned my back so she wouldn't see me. I was still mad that she had assumed I live in the Project.

Not that there is anything wrong with living there. Some very nice people, black and white, live there. What made me mad was that she automatically decided that because I was black, I lived there too.

I looked over my shoulder to check on Mrs. Sessions just in time to see her go into the main auditorium for the service. I was glad to see her disappear. With a little luck I could avoid her after church too.

A few minutes later, Mom, Dad, the boys, and I slid into our usual pew. Imagine my surprise to find Mrs. Sessions in the same pew, sitting beside a man who looked like a professional football player. She was as surprised to see me as I was to see her. I could tell because her jaw fell open for a minute.

We smiled sweetly at each other.

Partway through the service, Pastor Denning said, "I'm sure many of you folks are aware of the story of a special little girl in East Edge named

Melody. Because of the unusual circumstances that surround Melody, Dr. Eric Jackson, the chairman of our Board of Elders, has something to say on behalf of the Calvary Church leadership."

I watched with interest as Dad walked up front and stood behind the pulpit. I hadn't known he was going to say anything today. I couldn't resist glancing at Mrs. Sessions to see if she'd noticed that Dr. Jackson was my father.

Her jaw was hanging open again.

"Last week," said Dad, "the local papers were full of the story of Melody and her foster sister, Charlie Fowler, who rescued Melody when she was kidnapped. Included in the newspaper accounts of Melody and Charlie was the information that Melody is HIV-positive.

"Surely all of us grieve that a six-month-old baby faces life with a death sentence hanging over her. But this grief is more than the oh-my-how-terrible type because Melody is part of our church family as the foster daughter of our own Ann and Don Anderson."

Dad smiled at the congregation. "Most of you who are aware of Melody's situation have been very gracious, trusting the church leadership to handle the health aspects of this case as well as the spiritual aspects. But I must tell you with sorrow that at least one of us has reacted in a manner that it totally unacceptable to us as a group of Christians. This individual has written poison-pen notes to both Pastor Denning and to the Andersons."

There was a general murmur in the congregation. Dad waited a moment for it to die down.

"At first we were going to ignore this cowardly action, but when—through unexpected circumstances—several people learned about the poison-pen notes, we decided that the best way to defang the monster was to make all of you aware of its cowardly behavior.

"I stand before you this morning as a representative of the leaders of this congregation, and I say firmly that Pastor Denning and the elders of Calvary Church find both the notes and the note sender to be wrong. We want to remind you that Christ reached out to the lepers, and we today must reach out to those who are ill. As my daughter Alysha says, 'The Bible says we should love one another, and not just those who are well.' "

Dad looked at the four hundred people seated in front of him. "I know it can be scary to have someone who is HIV-positive in our church. Please

trust us to care for you as well as care for Melody.
Thank you."

Dad took his seat in the pew beside us. I was so
proud of him.

"Be careful of pride, Alysha," he always tells
me. "It can make you into an arrogant person."

I know he's right, and I know he says that to
me because he's a genius like I am, and he has a lot
of reason to be proud. Not only is he the first one
in the Jackson family to have a Ph.D.; he is also
the first man in the family to graduate from
college, the first to wear a white shirt to work, and
the first who could afford to build his own house.
The fact that he built our house near his parents
on the street where he grew up shows me that Dad
hasn't let himself become proud.

Now I grinned at Dad as he held out a
hymnbook for me to share with him. I decided
that it might be wrong for me to become proud
about myself, but it was all right for me to be
proud of him.

During the sermon I practiced my penmanship
and tried to count the number of hairs on the
head of the almost-bald man in front of me. Mom
had made certain Damon sat beside her and Thetis
sat on the other side of Dad. The boys didn't

exactly sit still, but at least they didn't embarrass me in front of Mrs. Sessions.

After church was over, I figured I couldn't ignore Mrs. Sessions again, so I did the right thing. I introduced her to my parents. She introduced us to the football-player guy, who was Mr. Sessions.

"Have you lived in East Edge long?" Dad asked.

"Just since the end of August," Mr. Sessions said. "I'm the new football coach at the high school."

At least I was right about him looking like a football player. Now that I was standing near him, I felt I'd get a stiff neck from talking to him, he was so tall. And full of muscles. I bet he had to get his clothes specially made.

"You must work for Cammi's father," I said. "Cammi Reston. She's my friend, and her dad's the high school principal."

Mr. Sessions smiled. "Nice guy."

We all nodded our heads and made little agreeing noises.

"He's around here somewhere," I said, looking for Mr. Reston in the after-church mob—not an easy task when you're my height. He could be two people away, and I'd never see him. When I noticed that nobody but me seemed to care where

Mr. Reston was, I stopped looking.

Instead I started watching Mrs. Sessions, and it was an amazing experience. She kept looking at Mr. Sessions, and she was all soft and misty-eyed and looked very pretty. Somehow I'd never have picked her to be the romantic type. It just proved to me again how much appearances can trick you.

We were all walking down the aisle when Mrs. Sessions put her hand on my arm.

"Alysha," she said, looking very serious. "I need to talk to you."

I stopped and waited.

She cleared her throat as if the words were caught and she had to *ahem* them loose.

"I owe you an apology. I made certain assumptions about you, and I realize now how wrong that was."

"You thought I lived in the Project."

She nodded. "I did, and I feel very bad about that." Again she cleared her throat. "I've always looked at myself as a person who wasn't prejudiced. It's been a terrible shock to realize that I'm not the person I thought."

I felt so weird listening to her. Not only was she talking to me the way she would talk to an adult, but she was also apologizing to me—something adults hardly ever do to kids.

"I'm a Christian, Alysha," she said. "I have been for many years. The subtle prejudice I showed toward you must have made the Lord very unhappy. Please forgive me."

Now it was my turn to clear my throat. I nodded and mumbled, "Don't worry. It's okay."

"Are you sure?" She looked at me closely.

I nodded again. What else could I do?

She nodded back and smiled. "I feel so much better!"

"Hey, Sally, honey, come on!"

Mrs. Sessions and I looked up and found Mr. Sessions signaling in our direction. I was afraid he was going to rip the shoulder seams of his jacket apart the way he was waving that huge arm. I hoped Sally Honey had lots of needles and thread. She was certainly going to need them.

Mrs. Sessions waved daintily to her husband. "I've got to go, Alysha. I'll see you at the gym tomorrow."

I watched her hurry away and sighed. I was going to have to stop disliking her now that she'd been so nice.

"Was that who I thought it was?" said a voice in my ear.

I turned to Bethany, who liked to sneak up on people, and said, "She's sort of nice, you know?"

Bethany and I spotted Charlie across the lobby outside the auditorium. There were lots of people walking around between us and her, so we started ducking elbows and avoiding little kids and moving in her direction.

I could see that there were people who were making a point of heading in the same direction we were. Only, of course, they weren't trying to get to Charlie, but to Mr. and Mrs. Anderson. I guess they were the ones who wanted to be extra nice since Dad had told about the poison-pen letters.

They shook the Andersons' hands and oohed and aahed over Melody, who smiled brightly back. She was the cutest little thing in her little blue dress and tights and shiny black shoes.

I also noticed some people who grabbed their kids and headed for the door farthest from the Andersons. I felt angry at all of them for Melody's sake.

Brooke walked past us, heading who knew where. As always she was dressed like she was sixteen instead of twelve. Today she actually had on black stockings with dressy heeled shoes. Of course the heels weren't very high, but they were definitely heels. And Brooke didn't even teeter in them.

Her dress was red with a white collar and a black belt and a black band around the bottom. I glanced at Bethany who had on pink slacks and a pink flowered shirt; then I looked down at my denim jumper and flats. Even considering Bethany's chest, nobody would ever mistake us for sixteen.

"Hey, Brooke," I called. "Where are you going?"

She spun around and looked at me, her lips pressed together in a thin line. She was upset about something.

"Home," she said sharply. She tucked her little clutch bag under her arm with determination. I always thought of Princess Diana every time I saw Brooke with that silly little purse. I could never figure out what she or Princess Di carried in something so small. I mean, why bother?

"You're not going home for a while," I said, pointing across the lobby. "Your parents are busy talking to the Andersons. In fact, your mom's holding Melody."

Brooke looked where I pointed and made a face as she saw Melody happily munching on her mother's pearls.

"She's too nice for her own good sometimes," she said.

"Who?" asked Bethany. "Mrs. Anderson?"

"Of course not." Brooke threw one of her I'm-sophisticated-you're-dumb looks at Bethany, but Bethany missed it completely. She was still watching Melody. "If Mrs. Anderson wants to hold that baby," continued Brooke, "it's up to her. I don't have to live with her. It's my mother I'm worried about!"

I felt anger towards Brooke and her terrible attitude.

"If I were you," I said tartly, "I wouldn't worry about your mom. I'd be proud of her."

Brooke sniffed as though my comment was beneath her notice, but I suddenly recognized real fear in her eyes.

"You're really worried about all this, aren't you?" I said, my anger turning to amazement and pity. "You're actually afraid your mother is going to become sick just because she's holding Melody."

"Anyone with half a brain is scared," she said, scowling at me.

"Come on over with us," I said. "You don't have to hold Melody. Just come close enough to see she's not dangerous."

"No!" Brooke jumped back as though I'd suggested that she put her hand in an open flame. She turned and fled down the hall and out the door at the far end of the building.

It was one of the very few times I'd ever felt sorry for her.

Bethany and I shook our heads at each other, then walked across the lobby to Charlie.

"How have things been this morning?" I asked her.

She smiled. It was nice to see her smiling again instead of looking so worried. "Most people have been very nice."

"Melody didn't go to the nursery, did she?" asked Bethany.

Charlie shook her head. "We sat out here." She pointed to the lobby. "The sound system in the auditorium is hooked up to play out here, so we can hear what's going on. We heard your father, Alysha. He was great."

I smiled. "Thanks."

Bethany turned and faced the auditorium. "You can't see what's going on inside from out here, can you?"

"No. They can't leave the door open because Melody is too noisy. There was another lady out here walking her crying baby too."

I made a face. "I have a hard enough time paying attention when I'm in the auditorium. How can you ever concentrate out here?"

"I'd want to spend all the time playing with Melody," said Bethany.

Charlie shrugged. "If it were up to me, we'd just stay home. But Mrs. Anderson says we have to come to church on Sunday. She says it's important to be in God's house." Charlie didn't look convinced. "I guess she knows what she's talking about, but it seems sort of dumb to me, sitting out here and not—"

"—not seeing anything," said Bethany with a nod.

It's funny how I forget that Charlie never went to church at all until about a month ago when she came to live with the Andersons. Being in church every Sunday sounds normal to me but not to her. Though I think I'd feel the same way she does about sitting in the lobby. Boring.

Mrs. Picardy stopped beside us. "Have you seen Brooke?" she asked.

I nodded. "She went out the far door. I guess she's waiting at the car."

Mrs. Picardy smiled sadly. "My poor baby," she murmured and followed Mr. Picardy outside.

"Now there's a new take on Brooke," said Bethany. "My poor baby." She snorted. "Only a mother."

"Only *some* mothers," said Charlie quietly.

Bethany and I looked quickly at Charlie, and Bethany turned red with embarrassment. She hadn't meant to remind Charlie that her mother had abandoned her.

"I'm sorry, Charlie," Bethany said.

Charlie just shrugged and nodded. "I'll get used to it someday. I guess."

As we stood there trying to figure out what to say next, Bethany's parents came and got her. Charlie turned to Melody, so I wandered off to find Damon and Thetis.

I hadn't gone very far when I bumped into

Edward. He was leaning against the wall, obviously waiting for Uncle James and Aunt Arlette. He looked bored and angry, like he couldn't wait to get out of there. Unfortunately for me, I made a good target for his impatience.

"Well, well," he said, "if it isn't little old Alysha." He looked over my shoulder, then all around us in a very exaggerated manner. "Where are all your little white friends?" he asked. "Have they dropped you? Or have you gotten smart and dropped them?" He gave me a nasty grin.

I just stared at him. Come to think of it, I stared at him a lot, mostly because I couldn't believe how dumb he was. I certainly wasn't going to give up Dee or Bethany or Morgan or Sasha on his say-so.

I wasn't going to give up any of the others in the Kids Care Club either, not Cammi with her soft heart and quick tears, not Shannon who accepted everyone and had grown so tall that the top of my head barely reached her armpit, not prickly Charlie who wanted you to think she didn't care what you thought but who really ached for you to like her. Hey, Edward had me so angry I wasn't even willing to give up Brooke.

"Edward," I said, trying to keep my temper, "I

hear you're a good student."

He looked confused. What did his grades have to do with anything? "So?" he snarled.

"So?" I looked at him in disbelief. "What kind of an answer is that? Are you or aren't you a good student?"

"I am," he said. "I have to be. My father won't let me be in the Screaming Eagles if I don't keep my grades up."

"The East Edge Drill Team," I corrected.

He looked disgusted. "Don't remind me. Why do you care about my grades?"

"Because I can't understand how someone who's supposed to be smart can ask such dumb questions about my friends!" My voice was loud and sharp.

"My, my," said Edward, delighted at my anger. "Touchy, aren't you? I must have hit a nerve."

"I've had a couple of hard days," I snapped. "Now get out of my way."

He grinned at me and refused to move. I had to push him aside, and his cackle followed me the whole way down the hall. In a red fury I stomped to the far door, threw it open, and marched to the parking lot, making believe I didn't hear him.

I absolutely hate to be laughed at!

I stalked to our car, planning to sulk in the backseat until Mom and Dad and the boys came. Instead I found a locked car.

"Great!" I roared to a pair of startled kids on their way to their car. "Who else's father locks his car in the church parking lot?"

I climbed onto the hood and sat, staring grumpily at nothing. But as usual I couldn't think only of one thing, and my anger at Edward quickly gave way to the puzzles of the past few days.

How could I possibly help Melody?

Could I really like Mrs. Sessions?

Was Edward right or wrong about racial issues?

And could he, my own cousin, be the writer of those nasty letters?

God, why does life have to be so difficult?

Eventually I got bored sitting on the car, and I walked back inside the church. Almost everyone was gone now, even the Andersons, but I wasn't surprised. Somehow we Jacksons were always one of the last families to leave Sunday after Sunday.

I spotted Mom and began walking toward her. Before I reached her, Mrs. Jack appeared, and the two of them started talking. Even at a distance I could tell it was going to be a long and serious conversation.

I'm always amazed at how many women pour out their problems to Mom. It's good, I guess, but it holds my life up sometimes. Like now. I sighed and headed for the bench along the wall, ignoring my growling stomach.

I looked around and saw Dad and the boys talking with Uncle James and Aunt Arlette just outside the main door. I could go and join them, but I didn't want to talk to so many people. I stayed where I was.

To my left the long hall stretched empty. I looked at it, then looked away. I looked back, then stared a few minutes. My palms got all itchy and my legs couldn't stay still. I was fidgeting worse than the boys.

It was an invitation I couldn't resist. I looked quickly around. There was no one in sight but Mom and Mrs. Jack, and they weren't paying any attention to me. I stood, took a deep breath and took off, cartwheeling right down the center of the hall.

It felt wonderful to get rid of some of my energy after sitting and thinking all morning.

I entered the little foyer at the far end of the hall on my hands and noticed something hanging on the glass door, but it wasn't until I had finished my final cartwheel and was back on my feet that I realized what I was seeing. I was looking at another poison-pen letter.

EAST EDGE KIDS CARE CLUB

I walked slowly to the door and opened it. I went outside and stared at the piece of notebook paper taped to the glass. Slowly I reached up and pulled it free.

Denning—

Think you can embarrass us into silence? Guess again! We want that baby out of here! OR ELSE!

I couldn't believe my eyes. After Dad's comments this morning, I expected that the poison pen would realize how wrong he or she was and give up. Was I wrong or what!

Suddenly it hit me that the note had been hung during a very narrow window of time. I had gone out of this very door to our car, found the car locked, and come back through this door. There had been no note then.

Next I had gone down the hall, seen Mom talking with Mrs. Jack and Dad talking with Uncle James and Aunt Arlette, and cartwheeled back down here almost immediately.

There were only a few minutes during which the note could have been hung.

I looked around, searching for someone slinking away, someone who looked guilty, someone who was guilty.

And I found someone. Edward.

He was hiding behind one of the few remaining cars, peering carefully around to see if anyone was watching him. He ducked his head a minute, then sprinted to the next car. He scanned the parking lot again, then ran up the drive and out onto the street, heading away from church. He didn't see me seeing him.

Edward! I was shocked and surprised, yet I wasn't. I was more mad than anything. How could he! My own cousin!

Without a second thought I took off after him. He couldn't be allowed to get away with such a terrible thing.

Poor Uncle James, I thought. He's going to be

so upset and disappointed. He has such great dreams for Edward. He wants Edward to do at least as well as my father has done, if not better. I'm not certain Edward understands this, but all the rest of the family does. I don't know about the others, but I'd always wondered privately if Edward was up to Uncle James's dreams. Now I guessed that I had my answer. Poor Uncle James.

Both Edward and I are good runners because of all our exercise, me at the gym and him with his drill team. We both have good endurance. When he cut into the parking lot at the strip mall that includes Jack's Bakery among its stores, neither of us had slackened our pace.

But I had gained on him because he didn't know I was chasing him. I ran faster than ever.

When Edward cut into the parking lot, he dodged behind a car and crouched. Then he raised up a bit and peered through the window, looking away from me. He ducked down again and sidled around that car and the one next to it. I couldn't imagine what in the world he was doing. Maybe it was a matter of once a sneak, always a sneak, even when it wasn't necessary to sneak.

"Edward!" I yelled.

He jumped and spun around, his eyes wide, his

mouth open in surprise.

"I know what you're up to!" I yelled. "How could you?"

"Alysha!" He turned and began running toward me. "Get out of here! You'll get in the way! You'll ruin everything!"

"I just bet I will!" I yelled as I ran at him as fast as I could.

When we got close to each other, he reached out and grabbed at me, but I was ready for him. I ducked under his arms and hit him in the stomach with my head. We both went tumbling in a mess of arms and legs.

I was surprised at how much it hurt to butt someone. It never seems to hurt anyone on TV, but it sure hurt me. As I lay on the ground shaking my head, clearing away the stars, I realized that Edward was in worse shape than I was. He was gasping and coughing and trying to breathe, sort of like the fish I catch when dad takes us fishing.

"How could you, Edward!" I had to yell to hear myself over the pounding in my ears. "I can't believe you were that low!" I got to my knees and loomed over him. He's a lot bigger than I am, but I was definitely in control at the moment. "Writing a note like that!"

He shook his head wildly and tried to talk, but all he could do was to make little choking sounds. Finally he had enough air to gasp, "Not me." Then he had a fit of coughing.

"Not you?" I narrowed my eyes, suddenly uncertain. "Not you?" Maybe Uncle James was going to enjoy today after all.

"In there," he whispered, curling in a ball, holding his stomach.

There was Jack's Bakery.

"You mean the letter writer went into Mr. Jack's?" I was appalled that someone could do something as terrible as write that note and then go buy some pastry as though nothing was wrong.

Edward stopped moaning long enough to manage a weak, "Yes."

I got to my feet and peered between the parked cars. Now that I stopped to think about it, I found it amazing that no one had noticed Edward and me rolling and thrashing on the ground. No one had asked what was going on, and no one had asked if we needed help.

Looking around, I decided it was because no one could see us down between the cars. Which might be good for two reasons. First, it would be extremely embarrassing to confess to head-butting

Edward by mistake, and secondly, the poison pen still didn't know we were after him or her.

I sneaked up to the front fender of the car we were behind and cased the parking lot the way they do on TV. All the cars were empty.

I looked at the front of Jack's Bakery. Inside there was someone who might be dangerous. At least it was someone who was warped.

I made a dash for the door just as it flew open. I was going so fast that I couldn't stop myself, and I ended up in another wild tangle of arms and legs. This time the tussle was made even more interesting by the chocolate cake that was getting ground into the sidewalk as I wrestled with the poison-pen writer.

In the brief flash before we collided, I had recognized the person coming out of Mr. Jack's door, and as I tried to wipe white frosting from my eyes, I thought sadly that it all made sense. Even so, I was very disappointed.

The writer was not a person of great courage—surprise, surprise—and she began screaming and shrieking under me.

"Alysha, what's going on?" said a loud voice in my icing-filled ear.

I was lifted into the air by strong arms and

shaken a couple of times. Dangling in the air with as much dignity as I could muster, I ignored my rescuer—it turned out to be Mr. Jack—and glared down into the face of Brooke Picardy.

She lay there amid the remains of a birthday cake, curled up in a little ball just like Edward. Her red dress was now decorated with lots of white icing, her black stockings had a huge run, and her curls drooped over her face. Brooke was messier than she had ever been in her life.

"She did it," I gasped. "She did it."

Brooke uncurled herself now that I was no longer on top of her. She sat up, looked at me, and howled, "I did not! You ran into me, Alysha! You ruined my grandmother's seventy-fifth birthday cake!"

I'd never seen anyone cry like Brooke. Somehow she looked quite pretty even with her scraggly hair and her dirty dress and her watery eyes. Somehow she also got all the sympathy while I stood there ignored.

"But she did it," I repeated as Mr. and Mrs. Picardy and Mr. Jack fell on their knees to help poor, delicate Brooke in her hour of need. I guess old Edward was still holding his stomach over behind the car.

"Poor Brooke," Mr. Jack said. "Come on in and get cleaned up. And don't worry. I've got a display cake that will be just perfect for your grandmother. Shush, now. It'll be all right."

Three pairs of hands set Brooke on her feet. She wobbled there for a minute in her heels. Then she looked at me with venom.

"You ran into me!" Brooke shrilled. "You did it on purpose!"

"I did not!" I countered.

"Yes, you did!"

"Did not!"

Brooke turned a pathetic face to Mrs. Picardy. "Mommy, look what she did to my dress! And Grandmom's cake!"

"What I did?" I shouted. "Do you know what she did?"

"Girls, girls!" Mrs. Picardy, her beautiful dress all slimy with icing, interrupted our shouting match. "Enough for now. We all need to get cleaned up."

"But—" protested Brooke.

"But—" I said.

"But nothing," Mrs. Picardy said. "I don't want to hear another word until we're all cleaned up."

Suddenly I understood why Brooke had shown

up to clean the church nursery. Her mother didn't speak very !oudly, but somehow we all did exactly what she said. Maybe it was because she was rich and lived in her big house and was used to giving orders to her help. I don't know.

I do know that Brooke and I weren't very happy to find ourselves in Mr. Jack's little bathroom together. We scowled at each other as Mrs. Picardy cleaned up first Brooke, then me, then herself. Every time either of us started to open her mouth, Mrs. Picardy just said, "Tut, tut," and we shut up. It was amazing.

I'd never had bakery icing smeared all over me before, and I was surprised at how hard it was to get off. Finally, though, we all paraded out, not exactly ready for a fashion show, but at least with clean faces.

"Feeling better?" It was Mr. Jack, looking at us kindly. It seemed to me he was trying not to laugh.

"Better," I mumbled.

"Better," Brooke mumbled.

"Wonderful," he said. "Brooke, your father has another cake for your grandmother in your car. I'm sure you will find it makes a fine replacement."

Brooke didn't look convinced.

"And Alysha, your cousin is out there on the curb, apparently not feeling well. I guess you were rushing in here to call for help when you bumped into Brooke. I called the church and got James. He and your father are coming for you and Edward."

"Oh, Alysha," Mrs. Picardy said, "is Edward going to be all right? Isn't it a shame, Brooke, that Edward's feeling so badly?"

Brooke looked at me thoughtfully. There was nothing slow about her, and she had to realize that Edward and I knew all about her. Now was her big opportunity. I waited for her confession with great interest.

"Don't worry about knocking me over and ruining my cake," she said sweetly. "I didn't like this dress much anyway."

As her mother patted her on the shoulder approvingly, I stared, too surprised to say anything. She had nerves of steel!

Before I knew what happened, the Picardys were gone.

Mr. Jack started to laugh. "That Brooke!" he said. "If she were mine, I'd be scared to death."

"You don't know the half of it," I said.

"Yeah," he said as he picked up a broom. "I can imagine."

"No, you can't. Let me tell you—"

"Not now, Alysha, I've got to clean up that mess out front before someone slips in it and sues me for a million bucks. While I'm busy, you just go behind the counter and help yourself to one of my super-sized cookies."

"Wait," I said, "I've got to tell you about—" but Mr. Jack was out the door. Sometime soon someone had better listen to me about Brooke, I thought, or I'm going to scream!

I went behind the counter for a cookie, making believe I worked here and was serving a very important customer. It was interesting looking at the store from back there. It looked different somehow. As I slid open the glass door on the back of the shelf, my mouth was watering. Forget the imaginary customer. This cookie was mine! It had been a very long time since breakfast.

Maybe my hands were a bit shaky from all the excitement. Maybe I was just careless. Anyway, as I lifted the cookie out, I knocked it against the edge of the door and it broke. Several pieces fell to the floor.

I looked at the little chunks lying there and wondered if I could just throw them out and take another cookie. I mean, I was certain Mr. Jack's floor was clean because he cooked in here and all, but a floor is still a floor.

Besides, wouldn't mice be attracted to a bakery? I would be if I were a mouse. It'd certainly be a nicer place to live than, say, a hardware store. I looked hard, but I couldn't see any mouse dirt or any other evidence of mice like mousetraps. Still, I wasn't about to eat those crumbs.

And I did want a cookie!

Muttering to myself, I turned and put the piece

left in my hand on the work counter by the cash register. I needed a dust brush and pan to get all the pieces up off the floor, so I started searching.

I looked in the cupboard under the cash register and found lots of junk. Mr. Jack wasn't very neat where the public couldn't see.

I pushed aside a box of the little papers the workers use to get cookies and stuff without touching them. I moved a roll of paper for the cash register and three half-empty cans of Mountain Dew. I looked under a pack of three-ring notebook paper and a couple of Bic pens. Nothing.

I went through the archway into the area behind the store. I felt weird going back there, almost like I was trespassing.

It was like entering a magical, forbidden garden with great expectations—and finding only weeds growing there. Of course Mr. Jack didn't have weeds. He had ovens and counters and cupboards, but none of them were being used. Maybe it was magical back there when the baking was going on, but it wasn't at the moment. In fact, it was sort of dreary.

I found a closet full of all kinds of cleaning tools, a dustpan and broom among them. I swept all the little cookie chunks into a pile and pushed them onto the dustpan. I noticed that I had collected some dirt along with the crumbs, and was glad I had decided not to eat the stuff off the floor.

But I still wanted a cookie.

I noticed a balled-up piece of notebook paper under the edge of the counter and swept that up too. Then I stood, took my full dustpan, and dumped it into the wastebasket beside the back counter. All the little cookie crumbs showered down on some other, uncrumpled pieces of notebook paper.

I started counting the number of wasted, never-to-be-eaten chocolate chips lying in the bottom of the wastebasket when a word from one of the sheets of paper under the chips jumped up and socked me in the stomach.

Denning.

Slowly I leaned down and shook the paper free of the crumbs. I straightened, feeling all stiff and funny, like an old lady who can't move right because she has arthritis or something. My hands shook as I read.

Denning—

Don't think I'm embarrassed or scared by what was said this morning. I'm not.

Get rid of her!

There was a big scribble through the words, as though the writer had decided he didn't like what he'd written.

I pulled out another paper.

Denning—

Don't make me laugh. You think you can scare me? Get rid of that baby!

There were lines through these words too, like the writer had decided again that it wasn't done right.

And it wasn't right. It wasn't right in lots of ways.

I looked out front through the plate glass window and saw my friend sweeping up the chocolate cake mess that Brooke and I had made. I felt sick as the puzzle pieces slipped neatly into place. I knew that finally I had found the real poison pen.

When Bethany and I discovered the first note on Friday, Mr. Jack had been at church delivering his pastries to our Sunday school class. When Edward found the second note on Saturday, Mr. Jack had been delivering his famous muffins and Danish to the meeting of the Sunday school teachers.

In the process, he had been making everyone think he was the most wonderful of men.

I knew, of course, that anyone at all could have mailed the letter to the Andersons. There was no sure way to tie that to Mr. Jack except by the paper and printing and stuff. That was probably enough.

I thought of Mrs. Jack talking to Mom. She had been very upset. Was that because she knew what was going on? Poor lady! Having a husband who did stuff like this was even worse than having a cousin like Edward.

Also, if Mrs. Jack was still at church talking to Mom, she couldn't have written these trial notes. Only Mr. Jack, who had come to church this morning and heard Dad, could have written them. He must have driven to the bakery right after church, written his notes, picked the best one, driven back to church, taped it to the door when he thought no one was looking, and driven back to the bakery.

And Edward had seen him do it.

Good grief! I suddenly thought. Did that make Edward a hero because he actually solved the mystery first? What a scary idea!

I looked out the window again at Mr. Jack. Why had he done it? I thought for minute and came to the conclusion that he had done it for the same reason Brooke or anyone reacted poorly to Melody: fear.

I sighed. I could understand being afraid. AIDS is a scary thing. I just couldn't understand being cruel as well.

I knew I couldn't face Mr. Jack. I was too disappointed. I picked up the notes—they might be needed as evidence—and walked through his clean and shiny kitchen to his back door and outside. Then I walked around the building and along the sidewalk until I came to Edward. I sat down beside him and waited for Dad and Uncle James.

I didn't take another cookie.

"Will the meeting of the Kids Care Club please come to order?" said Dee.

It was Saturday evening, and we were all slouched in our living room stuffing ourselves with four kinds of pizza, two flavors of chips, and almost everything on the market that's carbonated. A batch of vanilla brownies—isn't that a contradiction in terms?—and another of chocolate were baking for dessert.

"And don't think you're going to get any," I'd said to Damon and Thetis, who stood in the doorway watching as we cooked.

Damon looked disappointed, but Thetis just grinned his wonderful grin. He knew we'd give them each a piece of everything.

"Hey, Alysha," asked Bethany, "is Edward speaking to you yet?"

Everyone laughed, including me.

"Is Edward capable of speaking to anyone in more than gasps yet?" asked Dee.

One benefit of being dark-skinned that many people overlook is that no one can tell when you're blushing. I knew I'd never live down my now-famous head butt, but at least most people didn't realize how embarrassed I was about it. If they did, the teasing would be even worse.

Not that I regretted the actual head butt nearly as much as I regretted my faulty reasoning. Looking back, I couldn't believe I was dumb enough to think Edward was guilty. Edward! My cousin! Just because he's a jerk doesn't mean he's nasty. He is, after all, a Jackson.

And I'm supposed to be a genius.

He does treat me with a lot more respect now, though. He realizes he can't push me around just because he's bigger and older. They don't call me a tiger for nothing.

I guess I should feel more distressed about my conclusions concerning Brooke's guilt than I do. I'm working on it.

I feel plenty of distress over Mr. Jack.

"Honey," Mom keeps reminding me, "he's scared about something he can't control."

I know he is. And I know he's sorry. And I know he's apologized to the Andersons. And I know he's meeting with Pastor Denning every week and will probably turn out to be a much better Christian in the long run. It will just take me awhile to get over such a major disappointment. I'm not used to adults I like turning out to be something just short of criminal.

I mean, even Brooke was honest enough to say she was afraid instead of hiding behind anonymous notes.

But tonight was a night for fun with my friends. Dee tried to look businesslike, a difficult thing since she was holding a large piece of pepperoni pizza in one hand and a can of Coke in the other.

"Any new business?" she asked. "Any jobs or anything?"

All the KCs but me shook their heads.

"I don't have a job exactly," I said. "But I've got a suggestion."

"Great," said Dee. "We need something to do."

I put my pizza down and cleared my throat. "We all know that Charlie and the Andersons will have to sit in the lobby every Sunday because Melody can't go to the nursery and she's too noisy to take into church. It bothers me that they'll miss being part of church, and I've been trying to decide what we can do about it."

Charlie waved her hand and Dee called on her. "Mr. Anderson and I are going to go into the service from now on. Only Mrs. Anderson and Melody will stay in the lobby. I think it's because they think I need to go to church." She gave a funny little laugh.

"Well, you do," said Dee, always the pastor's daughter. "We all need to."

"Even Mrs. Anderson," I said. "So here's my idea for the Kids Care Club. Every Sunday one of us and our mom will take care of Melody in the lobby so that Mr. and Mrs. Anderson can both go to church with Charlie. My mom and I will start tomorrow."

At first no one said anything. Then everyone began to talk at once.

"We'll take next week," said Dee.

Cammi the Tenderhearted started to cry. "That's the best idea! I love it."

"Me, too. My mom and I will help," said Shannon.

"Us, too," said Bethany.

I sat back and listened and felt relieved. They liked my idea and wanted to be part of it. I'd washed some of the mud off my face that I'd splashed on when I took out Edward.

And we'd be serving the Lord, which would make everyone happy, especially Gail. The Bible does say to love one another, even those who aren't well.

You don't need to be afraid to meet someone with AIDS or the HIV virus.
You cannot get AIDS or HIV from:

- Toilets, doorknobs, telephones, or drinking fountains

- mosquitoes, flies, or any other insects

- donating blood

- kissing, hugging, or shaking hands

- sneezes or coughs

- swimming pools

- dishes, utensils, or food handled by a person with AIDS

If you know someone with AIDS or who is HIV-positive, or if you want to know more about AIDS, you can talk to your parents or a teacher, or call or write one of these organizations:

National HIV and AIDS Information Service Hotline
Department of Health and Human Services
(800) 342-2437
(800) 344-7432 (Spanish access)
(800) 243-7889 (Deaf access)

Pediatric AIDS Hotline
(212) 430-3333

American Foundation for AIDS Research
1515 Broadway, Suite 3601
New York, NY 10036-8901
(212) 526-4100

AIDS Task Force of National Council of Churches
475 Riverside Dr. Room 572
New York, NY 10115
(212) 870-2421

Presbyterian AIDS Network
The Rev. Jim Hedges
John Calvin Presbyterian Church
6501 Nebraska Ave.
Tampa, FL 33604
(813) 236-0941